BLACK LAGOON
ADVENTURES

SPECIAL EDITION

BOOKS 1–7

BLACK LAGOON
ADVENTURES

SPECIAL EDITION

BOOKS 1–7

By Mike Thaler
Illustrated by Jared Lee

SCHOLASTIC INC.
New York   Toronto   London   Auckland   Sydney
Mexico City   New Delhi   Hong Kong   Buenos Aires

ISBN 0-439-85201-3

The Class Trip from the Black Lagoon, ISBN 0-439-42927-7,
Text copyright © 2002 by Mike Thaler.
Illustrations copyright © 2002 by Jared D. Lee Studio, Inc.

The Talent Show from the Black Lagoon, ISBN 0-439-43894-2,
Text copyright © 2003 by Mike Thaler.
Illustrations copyright © 2003 by Jared D. Lee Studio, Inc.

The Class Election from the Black Lagoon, ISBN 0-439-55716-X,
Text copyright © 2003 by Mike Thaler.
Illustrations copyright © 2003 by Jared D. Lee Studio, Inc.

The Science Fair from the Black Lagoon, ISBN 0-439-55717-8,
Text copyright © 2004 by Mike Thaler.
Illustrations copyright © 2004 by Jared D. Lee Studio, Inc.

The Halloween Party from the Black Lagoon, ISBN 0-439-68075-1,
Text copyright © 2004 by Mike Thaler.
Illustrations copyright © 2004 by Jared D. Lee Studio, Inc.

The Field Day from the Black Lagoon, ISBN 0-439-68076-X,
Text copyright © 2005 by Mike Thaler.
Illustrations copyright © 2005 by Jared D. Lee Studio, Inc.

The School Carnival from the Black Lagoon, ISBN 0-439-80075-7,
Text copyright © 2005 by Mike Thaler.
Illustrations copyright © 2005 by Jared D. Lee Studio, Inc.

Cover illustration by Jared Lee
Cover design by Steve Scott

12 11 10 9 8 7 6 5 4 3 2 1   6 7 8 9 10/0

Printed in the U.S.A.   23

First compilation printing, January 2006

CONTENTS

THE
CLASS TRIP
FROM THE
BLACK LAGOON

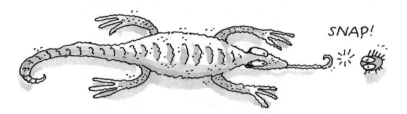

For Ruwan Jayatilleke,
a dedication to your dedication.
—M.T.

For Stephanie, Cassy, Zachery, Danielle, and
Garrett
—J.L.

CHAPTER 1

THE NEWS BLUES

We're going to take a class trip tomorrow. It's our first class trip. I hope it's a *first-class* trip!

I've read about the Titanic. Only the first-class passengers got the good food and lifeboats. I hope we don't hit a giant ice cube and go down the sink.

Maybe we won't take a boat at all. Maybe we'll fly on an airplane. I still don't know what holds those things up. Then again, maybe we'll take a train. I know what holds them up . . . bandits!

They say, "Getting there is half the fun." What's the other half? Getting back, of course!

CHAPTER 2
EXPLORING THE SUBJECT

In my history book, I learned a lot about some famous class trips. Lewis and Clark's class went across America. They couldn't find one open motel.

A kid named Chris Columbus sailed across the ocean. He got very seasick.

Marco Polo walked to China.
He met a real emperor.

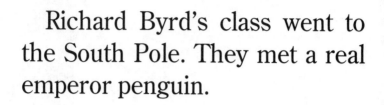

Richard Byrd's class went to the South Pole. They met a real emperor penguin.

QUACK!

WE COME IN PEACE.

And Neil Armstrong went all the way to the moon. He didn't meet anybody.

I wonder where we're going and whom we're going to meet.

19

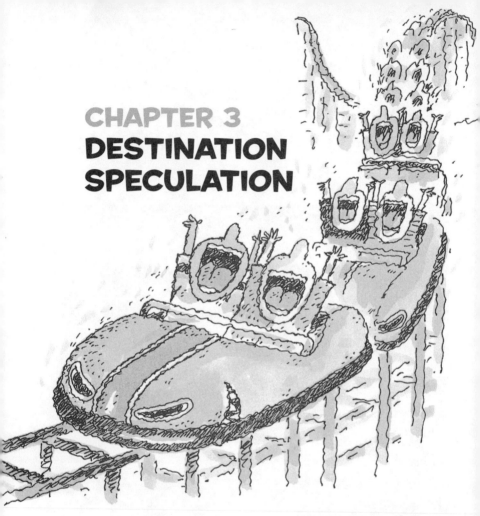

CHAPTER 3
DESTINATION SPECULATION

Freddy calls. We talk about all the possibilities. Then we pick our favorite one. Freddy wants to go to *Pizza Mutt*. I choose *Dizzyland*.

But we'll probably be going to
the nature museum or the art
museum. At one, you look at the
charts, and at the other, you look
at the arts.

Freddy still holds out for Pizza Mutt. He always looks on the bright side. He's an *optometrist*.

Then Eric calls. He always looks on the dark side. He's what they call a *messymist*.

He says that there's a 50-percent accident rate on class trips.

Half the class will be carried off by wild animals, fall off a high mountain, or drop into a deep hole. We choose our favorite. We both pick dropping into a deep hole, so we can pretend to be golf balls.

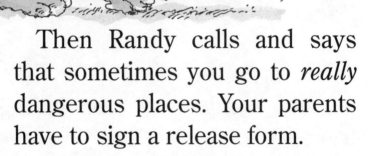

OUCH!

I HATE CATS!

Then Randy calls and says that sometimes you go to *really* dangerous places. Your parents have to sign a release form.

RELEASE FORM

One class went on a picnic to an active volcano. It erupted and all they ever found were 15 toasted peanut butter and jelly sandwiches.

25

Another class took a trip to Antarctica. Is there an *uncle-arctica* and *cousin-arcticas*? They're still defrosting.

My mom says that the first place I have to go is to bed because I have to get up early tomorrow morning.

CHAPTER 4
WONDER ENLIGHTENING

It's hard to fall asleep. I keep thinking about all the places we could go. And I worry about all the things that could happen.

We might make a journey to the center of the earth. But in the middle, it's like the hot fudge on a sundae.

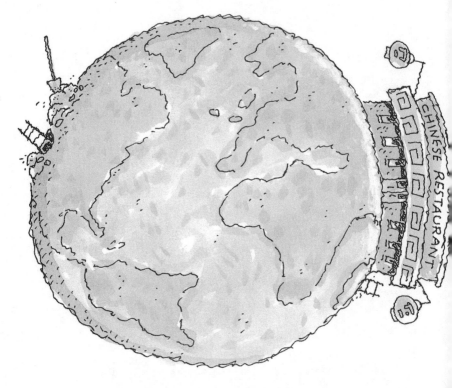

I don't even like to go into a closet. I'm happier when I can see the sky. Eric says I have *closet-ra-phobia*. If we go far enough, then we'll come out in China. Then we could eat lunch at a Chinese restaurant.

Or maybe we'll just go to the bottom of the ocean. There are many things down there with lots of teeth and lots of arms. It's also very dark. The deepest that I've ever been in the ocean is up to my ankles.

Maybe we'll go to Mars. They put you to sleep, and when you wake up . . . you're there.

The things on Mars are even weirder than the things at the bottom of the ocean.

They've got bigger teeth, longer arms like springs, and fingers like plungers. Their eyeballs are on stalks and wave around in the air. They all have bad breath and breathe through their ears. You have to put your head in a fishbowl and walk around in slow motion.

31

Where in the world are we going to go? Or where out of the world? I close my eyes and wonder. . . .

CHAPTER 5
THIS MUST BE D-DAY

The alarm goes off at 5:30 *in the morning*! I hate getting up early. The chickens aren't even up yet! And I shuffle into the bathroom.

My eyes are hardly open. I squeeze out some toothpaste and brush my teeth. Boy, it sure tastes weird. I look at the tube and it says BROWN SHOE POLISH.

My shirt feels very small. Then I discover that my head is in the sleeve. My pants feel odd, too. I discover they are on backward. At least I won't mess up with my shoes. Wrong again! I have the left one on my right foot. And the right one's on my knee. This is not going to be a great day.

CHAPTER 6
OFF WE GO

I wonder what I should pack. Randy says that you have to be prepared for anything. He says that he's taking snowshoes, malaria pills, signal flares, a snakebite kit, and a lifeboat.

I think I'll take my lucky rabbit's foot. Of course, it wasn't lucky for the rabbit.

Oh, well. I stumble downstairs for breakfast. I grab a box of cereal and pour some into a bowl. Then I pour in some milk. It all bubbles up. I look at the cereal box. It says DISHWASHING POWDER. . . . I guess I'll skip breakfast.

I open the front door and step outside. It's dark and full of coats. Wrong door. I try again and really step outside. It is just as dark but there are no coats. Even the early birds aren't up yet. I feel like an early worm and wiggle to the corner.

I wait there with my brown teeth chattering. Out of the gloom come two lights. It's the school bus. Mr. Fenderbender opens the door and I get on.

All the kids are there, sitting stiff and staring straight ahead. They all have brown teeth. Everybody's breath smells horrible. A green fog covers all the windows. I guess we won't be singing camp songs today.

After four minor collisions, Mr. Fenderbender stops and tells us to get out. Things have to get better . . . don't they?

CHAPTER 7
INTO THE WILD
BLUE YONDER

We're at a small airfield. Mrs.
Green is standing by the first
passenger plane ever made. It
says BUILT BY THE WRONG BROTHERS
on the side.

As we climb aboard, she hands each of us a parachute. I guess we're not going to the museum. We strap them on and try to sit in our seats. I feel like a camel.

Mr. Fenderbender puts on a pilot's cap with goggles and sits up front with Mrs. Green. They both try to figure out how to start the plane.

Meanwhile, Eric, the class clown, pretends to be the flight attendant and gives the safety instructions. "In case of the *likely* event of a water landing, your seat cushion can be used as a flotation unit." I look down. There is no seat cushion. This is definitely not first class.

Doris asks what movie will be playing. "We're showing a bunch of selected shorts," Eric answers. He smiles and then reaches into his backpack and pulls out his underwear. "Gross!" we yell.

45

Mr. Fenderbender guns the engine. We're all pressed back in our seats. "Happy landings," cackles Mrs. Green.

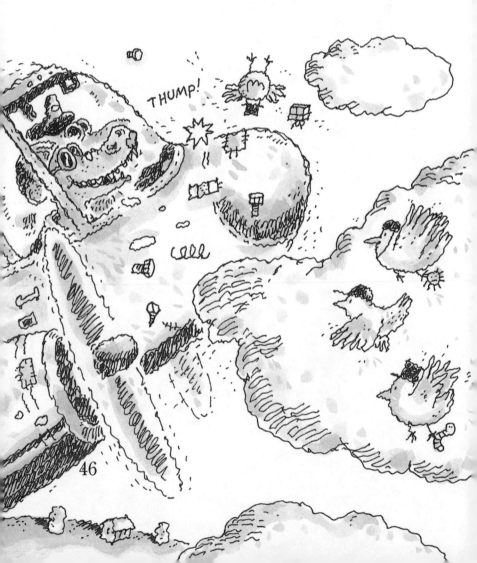

CHAPTER 8
FLYING HIGH

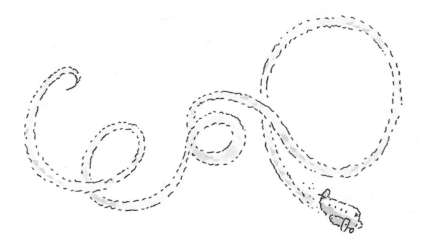

Mr. Fenderbender flies like he drives. We do loop-de-loops, barrel rolls, and dives. Penny throws up. Good thing I didn't eat breakfast.

After eight hours of aerial acrobatics, a red light goes on. Mrs. Green lines us up alphabetically, opens the door, checks our parachutes, and then pushes us out. Derek is first, but I'm secoooooooond!

We land all over—east, west, north, and south. There are kids twisted in every possible gymnastic position. Mrs. Green grades us on our landings. Freddy is the only one who gets an F. He landed in a lion's mouth.

We are all a little shorter as we line up and march off into the jungle. The lion burps. Freddy would have liked that.

CHAPTER 9
JUNGLE BUNGLE

The jungle is having a bad hair day. It takes every blade in my Swiss Army knife to hack our way through.

And you have to be *very* careful where you step. All the animals are party poopers, and you have to look out for the dreaded *hippo-potty-mess*.

The heat beats down on us. It's like being in a furry oven.

HALT!

All of a sudden, Eric shouts out, "Knock, knock!"

"Who's there?" we all ask.

Eric beats his chest and yells, "Tarzan!"

"Tarzan who?" we ask.

"Tarzan stripes forever!" he giggles.

I guess that's a little jungle joke.

A snake as long as a jumbo jet slides by. Hairy spiders as big as hamsters bounce on webs as large as trampolines.

Penny sniffs a purple flower
and it grabs the end of her nose.
Mrs. Green tells us the name of
the plant in Latin. She says we'll
have a quiz in an hour.

Randy sees a sandbox and jumps in. Unfortunately, it's a quicksand box. He sinks in up to his chin. "It's not recess yet," scolds Mrs. Green as she pulls him out.

Derek pets an orange zebra with black stripes. Mrs. Green tells him it's a tiger and that he doesn't have to raise his hand anymore if he has a question.

Mosquitoes as big as Count Dracula buzz all around us. They think it's lunchtime and that we're the special of the day. I feel like we're in an all-you-can-eat restaurant, and we're on the menu!

Eric shouts, "Knock, knock!"
"Who's there?" we all ask.
"Safari," he says.
We throw up our hands.
"Safari who?" we ask.
"Why do we have to walk safari?!" he laughs.

CHAPTER 10
FAST FOOD

Finally, we reach a river and cross it by stepping on crocodiles. One eats Doris's backpack and all. I guess that's the toll. It's sort of a potluck dinner. Without any luck . . . we'll be the dinner. I hope that a giraffe doesn't swallow me. The fall could be huge—or worse, I could be sucked up an elephant's nose. *Snot* a nice way to go!

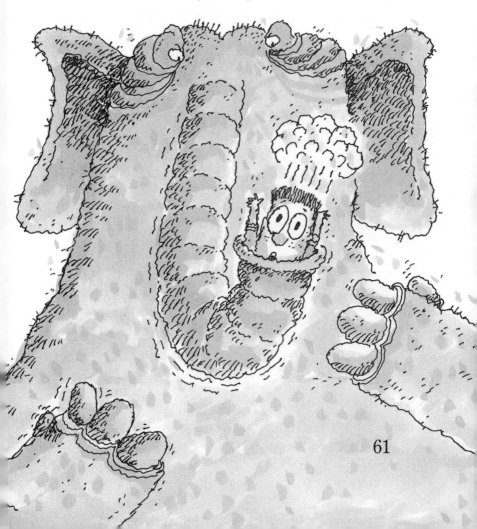

I don't want to be a baboon's breakfast, a lion's lunch, a crocodile's dinner, or a snake's snack. I run and hold up a sign that says PLEASE DON'T FEED THE ANIMALS. I hope they can read.

CHAPTER 11
IN THE GRAND SAND

By noon, we come to a desert. The good news is there's no more jungle. The bad news is there's a lot of sand. We're very thirsty. Unfortunately, there are no public water fountains. The only good thing about a desert is that if you add another *s* it would be a *dessert*!

63

Kids are dropping like flies.
I've never seen a fly drop, but
I've seen fly droppings. Anyway,
it's hot, and it's lunchtime.

I even miss the school
cafeteria. I'm losing it. I ask if we
can stop and eat. "Not until the
lunch bell rings," says Mrs.
Green. I hear a lot of bells.

Then I start seeing things. . . .
A Pizza Mutt wiggling in the heat
waves. A swimming pool full of
rubber ducks.

I even see a school bus. Wait, it
is a school bus! It drives up.
On the front of it are printed
the words **CLASS TRIP**.

Mr. Fenderbender opens the door and I get on. All the kids are sitting there bright-eyed and excited.

Mrs. Green says we're going to the zoo to see a lot of wild animals. Hey, that's baby stuff. They're all in cages. A zoo is pretty tame after you've seen the real thing.

Maybe next time we'll blast off to a space station, climb Mount Everest, or water-ski up the Amazon River.

Now *that* would be a *trip*!

THE
TALENT SHOW
FROM THE
BLACK LAGOON

To Alan Boyko,
My FAIR-haired friend
—M.T.

To Mom, who always reminded her young son
that his talent was a gift from God.
—J.L.

CHAPTER 1
THE SHOW *MUST GO ON*

We're having a talent show. I've heard all about them. Ten hours of endless embarrassment and nonstop nausea. And that's just for the audience.

But it's a lot worse for the performers! Some people never recover their shattered egos.

But Mrs. Green says every one
of us has to do something. She
says we must be onstage for at
least a minute, and not longer
than an hour. I *really* want to be
on the stage . . . yeah, the *first
stage* out of town.

On our way home, I ask my pals what they're going to do. Eric says that he's going to tell jokes. He'll be some sort of a stand-up *comic-kazi*. I'm sure we've heard all his jokes already.

Freddy says he's going to recite his recipe for apple turnovers. Derek is going to spin a hula hoop. Randy will perform his most mystifying magic trick. He's going to pull his head out of a hat!

77

Penny is excited to lip-sync
Beethoven's 9ᵗʰ Symphony!

And Doris, who takes ballet
lessons, says she's going to
dance the dying swan from *Swine
Luck*—or something like that.

79

Everyone asks me what I'm going to do. I just stare out the foggy window and mumble, "You'll see."

CHAPTER 3
STAR BRIGHT

What am I going to do?

My major talents are very specialized. I'm a great burper. I can burp "Yankee Doodle" after drinking a soda.

82

I can wiggle my ears and cross my eyes at the same time. I can touch the tip of my nose with the end of my tongue. But Freddy can pick his nose!

I can squirt milk out of my nose.
I did at Thanksgiving, but no one
applauded.

I can make my armpits quack like a duck.

QUACK

QUACK

QUACK

QUACK

I can stand upside down if someone holds my feet. Or I can stand right side up if there's a floor.

I can tie my body in a knot. But it takes an hour to get it untied!

I can make a *pigzilla* monster face! Or do my Count Dracula imitation!

I can blow in a bottle and sound
like a foghorn.

I just don't know what to do . . . I
have so many talents.

CHAPTER 4

MOTHER KNOWS BEST

I share my problem with my mom. BIG MISTAKE! She decides to help me.

HA HA HA HA HA

She suggests that I do a nice little dance. NEVER! Then she says I have a sweet singing voice. FORGET IT! Next, she tells me that I have a nice smile. Couldn't I just smile for a minute? I DON'T THINK SO!

Now she really puts on her thinking cap. I'm in big trouble! "I know," she says. "You can learn how to play the piano." And before I can throw up or even yell, she's already calling Mrs. Fumble, the piano teacher. Oh, great, now I have to take piano lessons!

CHAPTER 5

TREBLE TROUBLE

The first lesson is a complete disaster. I have two left hands and they're all thumbs. I finally find the middle C and hit it with my elbow.

Mrs. Fumble wears tons of perfume. She smells like a flower show. I will smell like a wedding for a week.

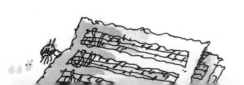

She's as big as a wrestler and always sits on the little piano bench with me. I can hardly see around her. And my side of the bench keeps lifting up in the air. She asks me why I want to play the piano. I say, "I don't. I'd rather be playing baseball."

My mom says that one day I will be the hit of the party when I sit down to play. I don't want to be the hit of the party. I just want to get through one minute onstage.

CHAPTER 6
KEY BORED

Instead of playing baseball, building race-car models, or going swimming and becoming a swordfish . . . here I am still practicing. This is hard.

CHING   CHING   CHING

I have to play the same thing
over and over for a whole hour.
And what makes things worse—
I have to listen to it.

CHING
CHING   CHING   CHING
CHING
CHING
CHING
CHING
CHING
CHING

CHING   CHING

The only good thing about playing the piano is that you can do it sitting down. After four weeks, five lessons, and thousands of hours of practicing, I can now play "Chopsticks." The good news is it takes just about a minute to play.

CHAPTER 7

SHOW BIZ GOSSIP

I call all the other kids to hear how they're doing. Eric tells me all his jokes. I've heard them before. And they're about as funny as a math test.

Freddy shares his recipe for apple turnovers. It sounds like the only thing it will turn over is your stomach.

Derek says he's a little bit dizzy from all the hula-hooping. Randy the Magnificent tells me that great magicians never give away their tricks.

Penny says her lips are in a cast. She sprained them practicing. And Doris asks me if I have any feathers for her costume.

103

This is going to be quite a show.
I can see it now . . .

CHAPTER 8
STAGE STRUCK OUT

The auditorium lights dim. The spotlight falls on Eric. But it doesn't hurt him. He gets up and tells his first joke. No one laughs. He tries a second joke. Again, no one laughs. Here comes his third joke. It's about the principal. Everyone laughs and he gets sent to the principal's office.

Then a hush falls over the audience. Freddy, who's wearing a chef's hat, opens his cookbook and reads the recipe for apple turnovers. Everyone's mouth is watering. It's close to lunchtime.

Then Randy comes out. He's wearing a magician's hat. He tells the audience that he's going to pull a human head out of it. There's a slow drumroll. And he pulls the hat off his head, bows, and walks quickly off the stage. Everyone is mystified!

Now Derek comes out. He's wearing a hula hoop. He spins it once and it spirals down to his feet. Everyone boos. He lifts up the hula hoop and tries again. It drops straight to the floor. But Derek doesn't give up. He keeps trying for an hour. Finally, Mrs. Green comes out and pulls him off the stage with the hoop.

BOO

BOO

BOO

109

Penny walks onstage. Her lips are out of the cast. Soon, the CD is playing, and we have to wait four movements until people start singing. But when they finally do, the CD starts skipping. Penny starts to cry and skips offstage. I hope there's not a talent scout in the audience.

The lights on the stage turn blue, and Doris comes out covered in feathers. She spins around, but her feathers begin to fly off and float over the audience.

Dying Swan is right. When she's done, she's ready for the oven.

Then it's my turn. Mr. Smudge, the school janitor, rolls out a concert grand piano. I come out and bow politely. I sit down at the keyboard and lift my hands. My two fingers are poised in the air. Suddenly, everyone begins sniffing and holding their noses. The entire auditorium is filled with the scent of lilacs—shades of Mrs. Fumble.

114

Soon, everyone runs outside to get a breath of fresh air. I'm sitting at the piano alone—all that practicing for nothing.

Suddenly, I wake up. It's time for bed. I can't believe the talent show's tomorrow.

CHAPTER 9
IT'S CURTAINS

That night, I have a dream. Well, more like a nightmare.

There's a bright stage and millions of people are sitting out in the audience. I'm standing in the middle of the stage. I can hear them all breathing. I'm wearing a purple tuxedo with a silver bow tie.

I take off my pink top hat. I announce that I will pull a live rabbit out of my top hat. There's a slow drumroll as I reach into the hat and pull out a mouse. Everyone shouts, "That's not a rabbit!"

I reach back in the hat and pull out a cat. The audience yells, "That's not a rabbit, either!"

BOO

118

I keep on trying the trick until the stage looks like Noah's Ark. Everything from aardvarks to zebras—but not one rabbit. Everyone boos and then throws carrots at me. And finally, the curtain comes down.

CHAPTER 10
A STAR IS BORN

Well, it's ten A.M. Showtime!

Everyone in school fills the auditorium. Little kids, big kids, teachers, and relatives—all expecting to be entertained. We huddle together backstage. Doris is in her feathers. Freddy is in his chef's hat. Penny is wearing lipstick. Randy is in his magician's hat. And Eric is wearing a red ball on his nose. That's funny stuff!

The lights slowly dim, the curtain rises, and we point to Eric. He's first. He steps out on the stage. All eyes are on him. He taps the microphone. It sounds like elephants on a giant trampoline.

He clears his throat and tells his first joke. Everyone laughs.

They applaud when Freddy reads his recipe. And they gasp when Randy takes off his hat and pulls out Waldo, our class hamster.

Derek has tied his hoop to his belt. And he spins around!

CLAP

CLAP

CLAP

CLAP

Penny lip-syncs "Girls Just Wanna Have Fun." And everyone in the audience wants to have fun, too!

CLAP

CLAP

CLAP

Doris gets through her dance, only losing three feathers. That's certainly a feather in her cap.

CLAP

CLAP

CLAP

Mr. Smudge slowly rolls out the piano. I come out and sit down. Then I take off my shoes and my socks.

CLAP CLAP   Bravo Bravo

I play "Chopsticks" like it's never been played before . . . with my toes! And the audience goes wild.

CLAP CLAP

CLAP CLAP

We're a hit! I have snatched victory from the *toes of defeat.*

This is my first step to stardom. I hope we can have another talent show next week. I will play "Chopsticks" with my elbows. I am just getting warmed up.

THE
CLASS ELECTION
FROM THE
BLACK LAGOON

To Dennis Adler,
who makes *Heaven and Mirth* real
—M.T.

A salute to all the men and women
in our armed forces
—J.L.

CHAPTER 1
ELECTION FEVER

We're having a class election. Mrs. Green says everyone has to run for something. I'd like to run for the hills. Maybe I can just let my nose run.

I don't want to be vice president because all they do is give advice. And I don't want to be secretary. You just spend hours keeping minutes.

And I don't want to be treasurer—I'm not so good at math.

I guess I'll run for president. Maybe they'll put my face on Mount Rushmore or on a three-dollar bill.

CHAPTER 2
CANDIED-DATES

Mrs. Green says we'll vote in two weeks and that we have to campaign and give speeches. This is going to be a cam*paign* in the neck. We may even have a debate.

Uh-oh, Doris is running against me. She says she wants to be the first woman president ever. That would make *me* the first loser ever.

Penny is going to be her campaign manager. Eric says that he'll be mine because he'd hate to see me lose to a girl.

Freddy wants to be *vice* president because the *vise* is his favorite tool in woodshop. Derek wants to be secretary because it has "s-e-c-r-e-t" in it. And Randy is running for treasurer because he thinks he'll get to keep all the money.

This is going to be a tough election.

139

CHAPTER 3

A FAST SLOGAN

Eric says that we need a campaign slogan.

"What about—*Vote for me?*" I say.

"Not enough pizzazz," says Eric.

I scratch my head.

"What about—*I'm a resident, make me president?*" I ask.

"Better," says Eric.

"Whoa, I think I have it. What about—*Don't be a booby, vote for Hubie?!*" I shout.

"Bingo!" cheers Eric.

140

141

"Now we need some posters. Doris already has some up in the hall," Eric adds.

"What's her slogan?" I ask.

"It's time for a change," Eric smiles.

"Sounds like a diaper ad," I laugh.

CHAPTER 4
OFF THE WALL

I'm not a great artist, but I can draw good dinosaurs. So I draw a T-Rex on five posters and print out my slogan.

Then Eric and I tape them up in the hall—next to Doris's posters. Doris even has one up in the boys' bathroom. Now, that's dirty politics. Someone's a traitor.

So I sneak into the girls'
bathroom and put up a poster.
Great causes take great risks. If
I get caught, it could ruin my
political career.

I can see it now. I am running
for President of the United
States. I'm ahead in the polls.

Then the story of how I snuck into the girls' bathroom is leaked. I'm all washed up in politics. My campaign stalls. My career goes down the drain. I'll never be flushed with victory.

Hey, their bathroom looks just like ours—what's the big deal?

CHAPTER 5
PRESIDENTS'
PRECEDENCE

I go to the library, and Mrs. Beamster shows me a book about past presidents. There were lots of them and they were *all* famous.

The first was George Washington, D.C. He never told a lie because he had wooden teeth. He couldn't lie through his teeth. That's why a bridge is named after him.

146

YOU HAVE A NICE SMILE.

Then there was Abraham Lincoln. He didn't lie, either. Mrs. Beamster says that he walked ten miles just to return an overdue book. He lived in Gettysburg because they said he had a Gettysburg Address!

Then there was Teddy Roosevelt. He invented the teddy bear. I heard he belonged to a motorcycle gang called The Rough Riders. And they won the San Juan Hill climb.

Mrs. Beamster says that all the presidents were great men. And if I win the election, I'd be in good company. Yeah, but none of them had to run against girls!

CHAPTER 6
A PEACH OF A SPEECH

After school, Eric and I go to my house. It's time to write the speech. I'm inspired.

"My fellow students . . ." I begin.

"No good," says Eric. "You have to try and steal the girl vote."

"Dear girls and boys . . ." I start again.

"But you don't want to lose the boy vote," says Eric, folding his arms. He waits patiently.

I clear my throat and say, "Dear voters . . ."

"Good. Now, what's your platform?" asks Eric.

"I don't need a platform," I reply. "I'm tall enough."

"No, no, what do you stand for?" asks Eric.

I put my hand over my heart. "The national anthem," I reply.

Eric raises his arms and sighs.

GRRRR...

153

"No, no, what's your agenda?" Eric says impatiently.

"My gender's a boy," I laugh. Eric rolls his eyes.

"No, no, what will you do if you get elected?" He huffs and puffs.

"Be surprised," I smile.

CHAPTER 7

A SPECIAL DELIVERY

Well, I finally write my speech, but then I have to give it. I stand in front of the mirror and start, "Dear voters..."

"From the heart," says Eric.

"Deeeeer voters..." I sing.

"Good," smiles Eric. And he pats me on the back.

I puff out my chest, fold my arms, and cross my eyebrows.

"Deeeeer voters, I stand before you today, so I'll be tall enough. Tall enough to reach the high office of president—a president of the people, by the people, and for the people. A

president that will stand by you, sit by you, and walk by you—in the cafeteria, in the classroom, in the bathroom, on the playground, I'll be there. So next week—don't be a booby, vote for Hubie."

Eric gives me a standing ovation.

CHAPTER 8
DREAMS OF GLORY

I'm beginning to like this. What if I win?

What if I go on to become President of the United States?

I would go and live in the White House. Maybe I'll paint it green. Then it would be the Green House, and I could grow orchids. Then I'd have an *orchid-stra*.

I could do a lot of good for everybody. I would end global warming, war, and hunger. I would put a pizza place in every town and village. I would make recess longer and math class shorter.

I would outlaw spinach and ban brussels sprouts. I would make the U.S. Mint—the U.S. Mint-chocolate chip. I would make the weekend six days, and the summer ten months. I would change the eagle to a beagle and make my dog the national symbol.

I would be famous. I'd have my own limousine, airplane, and skateboard. They would name things after me—Hubie Airport, Lake Hubie, and Hubieville.

I would go down in history ... if I win.

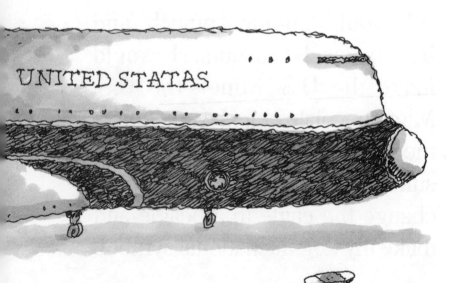

UNITED STATAS

CHAPTER 9
THE BALLOT OF HUBIE COOL

But what if I *lose*? To a girl? To Doris? What a bummer!

I can see it now . . .

None of my friends would ever talk to me again.

No one would sit at my lunch table. I'd eat alone for the rest of my life. I couldn't ask anyone to pass the ketchup.

I wouldn't be popular—I'd be *poop-ular*.

I'd be kicked off the baseball team and have to turn in my little league cap. I would have let down every boy in school and unborn generations of boys. I couldn't join the Boy Scouts.

I'd better start campaigning . . . now!

165

CHAPTER 10

A SHAKE-UP

"Now you have to go out, kiss babies, and shake hands," says Eric.

"Babies can't vote! There aren't even any in school," I answer.

"True, but there are lots of hands," smiles Eric.

166

Okay, so I go around and shake everybody's hand. I feel silly.

I shake Mrs. Green's claw and Coach Kong's paw. I shake, rattle, and roll.

DON'T BE A BOOBY VOTE FOR HUBIE

167

I even shake hands with Fester Smudge. This can't be very sanitary.

ZAP!

Then I go and have a milk shake.

CHAPTER 11
THE GREAT DEBATE

Well, Doris and I are in front of the whole class. I feel like I'm under a microscope. I should have combed my hair more, but Doris has a pimple on the end of her nose.

We shake hands and she goes first. She says that she's for women's rights and total equality. I ask her why she gets to go first.

"Because I'm a girl, of course," she sneers.

"Oh," I reply.

171

Then it's my turn. "Knock, knock!"

"Who's there?" says everyone.

"Debate," I answer.

"Debate who?!" shouts the class.

"Put debate on the hook and we'll go fishing!" I laugh.

"That's not funny," says Doris, poking me in the back.

172

"Is too," says I, poking her back.

"Is not," says Doris, stamping her foot.

"Is," I say, stamping mine.

"Not," says Doris, crossing her eyes.

"Is," says I, crossing mine.

We go on until the lunch bell rings and ends our debate.

CHAPTER 12
DORIS'S COOL MOVE

Unfair, unfair!

Doris says she's the candidate of the *Birthday Party*. She's buying ice cream bars for all the voters at lunch.

Everyone's lining up in drooling droves. My whole class. My best friends. Even Eric, my manager!

I'm betrayed in the cafeteria. I feel like that ancient Roman Emperor Julius Caesar Salad. Jabbed in the back with a dessert spoon. I feel *desserted*.

This is sweet-tooth politics. Underhanded. Underfooted. Underrated!

How can she stoop so low?

I better hurry before all the chocolate's gone!

CHAPTER 13
POLL POSITION

Yum, that was good. Now what can I do?

With my allowance, I couldn't afford to give out water. Anyway, I'm not going to buy votes. I'm going to stand on my principal. He may get angry, though.

I can't let Doris get ahead in the polls. The polls tell how people are planning to vote. I could climb the flag *poll*.

I could buy a horse and win the gallop *poll*. I could go to Antarctica and visit the South *Poll*. I could even go to *Poll*-land with a fishing *poll*.

How can I *poll* vault ahead? I have to do something to give Doris her just desserts.

I'M AHEAD.

179

CHAPTER 14
TAKING A STAND

I need to do something outstanding—something awesome, something that betters the school. But what?

I could mow the grass and have a lawn sale. I could rename the gym . . . Ted. I could take home plate home and put it in the dishwasher.

180

181

Wow! All the kids have dropped their ice cream wrappers on the floor. I'll pick them up. I'll be an environmental hero. I'll be the candidate of the *Mrs. Green Party*! I'll save the planet. This feels good.

Now I do stand for something.

ELECTION JITTERS

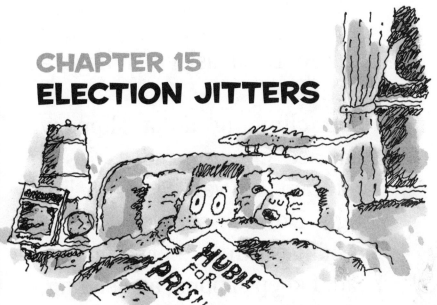

The pre-election night is a rough one. What if no one votes for me? Not even the boys. What if I lose by a landslide?

The power of ice cream is awesome. If I vote for myself, at least I'll have one vote. But everyone will know whose it is. Eric got two ice cream bars. Even he may not vote for me.

When I fall asleep, I have a nightmare . . .

I'm climbing up a slippery giant ice cream sundae. It's a mountain of vanilla with hot fudge. Doris is sitting on top—laughing, with a cherry on her head. I keep slipping and sliding, and she keeps laughing louder and louder until finally there's a thunderous roar. And I'm covered in a vanilla landslide.

I wake up and my head's under my pillow. It's Election Day!

Z-Z-Z

CHAPTER 16
HIGH NOON

Mrs. Green passes out pieces
of paper. I'm ready to pass out
with nervousness. It's a secret
ballot.

Doris looks very confident.
She's got a box of doughnuts for

her victory party—chocolate-coconut. I really hope that everyone doesn't drop his or her napkins on the floor.

Well, I'm voting for me — doughnuts or not.

Mrs. Green collects the ballots. Our names are written on the chalkboard. Doris and I are on top. Mrs. Green marks one vote for Doris. I hope that's Doris's vote. Then she marks another vote for Doris. That's probably Freddy's. He can't resist chocolate-coconut.

Then she marks one vote for me. That's probably mine. I wonder if Doris will let me come to her victory party. Then she marks another vote for me!

GRRR.

VOTE

WINK.

Eric winks.

Wow! We're tied. It won't be a landslide after all. Mrs. Green marks another vote for me. And another. And another. I can't believe it!

When all the votes are counted... I've won. I'm president! I can throw out the first ball in the little league game.

VICTORY

KING OF THE HILL

I look over at Doris. She has a tear in her eye. I go over and give her my last clean tissue. We shake hands.

She opens up her box of doughnuts and offers me one. She really has class. I want her in my cabinet, or even better—I'll make her my first lady!

THE
SCIENCE FAIR
FROM THE
BLACK LAGOON

To Jarryd Hasfurther,
a hero of faith
—M.T.

To all those science geeks in the past
who make our lives easier today
—J.L.

CHAPTER 1
IN THE BEGINNING

Mrs. Green says that we're going to have a science fair, and that we all have to invent something. I know all about inventors . . . I've seen them in the movies.

Inventors are a bunch of clowns with crazy hairdos, pop-bottle glasses, and baggy white coats. They are always trying to figure out ways to turn the world upside down!

NORTH POLE

WOW!

Some inventors and scientists make monsters like *Dr. Franky Stein*. Some turn themselves into monsters like *Jacqueline Hyde*, who thought two heads were better than one.

What about *Dr. Buzz*? He turned himself into a giant fly. He was flying high until he got zapped by a S.W.A.T. team. Or *Dr. Dill*on, who turned himself into a giant pickle!

Then there are those scientists who just *grow* things in test tubes, like prime slime, glob blob, and muck yuck. They always get stuck late at the office and are totally absorbed in their work. I wonder if I'll get wrapped up in my invention.

SPLAT!

CHAPTER 2
INVENTION INTENTION

What will I invent?

When I get home, I put on my thinking cap. The wheel's been done. It's been *around* for years. And someone's had the bright idea to make the lightbulb. It's not fair. All the good inventions have been invented already.

Eric calls while I'm trying to figure it all out. He says he's going to make a Frankenstein monster. He wants to know whether I want to collect body parts with him.

I ask him where he's going to get them. He says that he's going to a body shop or a parts department. I tell him that I've got problems of my own, but I hope someone gives him a leg up, lends him a hand, or helps him get a*head*!

GLUE

HAIR

BANG
BANG
BANG

203

When I hang up, I'm still scratching my head. Then Derek calls. He says that he's going to make himself invisible.

"Outta sight!" I say.

"Yeah, I'll be able to get into the movies for free, steal lots of bases in Little League, and hang out in the teachers' lounge."

I tell him that I'll see him later.

I still don't have a clue what to do. Soon Doris calls and announces that she's going to win first prize with her invention. She tells me there have been oodles of great women scientists.

"Name one," I say.

"Madame Curious," she answers.

"What did she do?" I ask.

"She discovered radiators," Doris replies.

Then I ask Doris what her project is, and she asks me if I have security clearance. "I don't think so," I say. So she hangs up.

I'm still scratching my head when Freddy calls. He has a big-*time* idea. He's going to make a time machine and send himself into the future so he'll be old enough to drive.

Freddy also tells me that Penny is making a telescope and Randy is building a rocket.

I've got no idea what I'm going to do. Maybe I'll clone myself. Who knows?

RULES
1. TAKE OFF YOUR GLASSES.
2. NO FOOD OR SODA ALLOWED.
3. UNTIE YOUR SHOES.
4. HOLD ANY LOOSE CHANGE.
5. NO TALKING.
6. YOU MUST BE THIS TALL.

TIME MACHINE

ENTER

NO ADULTS

ON → o
OFF → o

NO PETS

209

CHAPTER 3
THE CLASS CLONE

If I had a clone, life would be twice as much fun. He could do my homework for me. He could get up early and go to school while I stayed in bed. He could do my chores around the house and always eat my broccoli and spinach at dinner.

He could even take my piano lesson and practice while I play baseball. Or he could be on my Little League team and help me make double plays. He could go to bed early while I stay up late. It would be great!

Plus, my clone could go to the dentist for me. He could get all my vaccinations and take my medicine when I get sick. Boy, if I had a clone, life would be twice as much fun . . . for me!

CHAPTER 4
DOCTOR BRAIN

I FEEL SMARTER ALREADY!

Mom asks me to take out the garbage. Where's my clone when I need him?

Then I have an idea. If I'm going to be a scientist, I have to look like one. So I mess up my hair—good start. I put on my trick glasses with the funny eyeballs—even better. Then I put on my mom's white coat—I'm there!

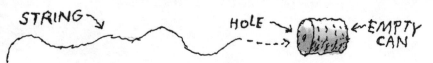

I look in the mirror and see a scientist looking back.

"Eureka! I've arrived!" I shout. There's a zingin' in my brain. Now I have lots of ideas!

I can make telephones out of two tin cans connected by a string. It would work for local calls. For long-distance calls, I'll just get a longer string.

I could make antigravity slippers out of banana peels, eyeballs out of eggshells, or roller skates out of apple cores.

Maybe I'll build a rocket, but that would make a lot of racket. I could create gum that quietly chews itself while you're in class! Or I could even make a TV remote that opens a book.

I could make a robot that rows a rowboat. I'll call him *Robert the Rowboat Robot.* It's a good tongue twister, anyway.

I'm too confused to choose. Cloning still leads the pack, but maybe I'll make a laugh machine.

ROW
ROW
ROW

216

CHAPTER 5
A SCI-FIVE

I turn on the TV and start watching the Sci Fi Channel. Mom tells me to do my homework. I tell her that I'm doing research!

There's a movie on called
Invasion of the Potty Snatchers.
It's about these Martians that
come to Earth to steal all the
toilets. I hope it has a happy
ending.

At the end of the movie, the Martians flip their lids, learn to play kazoos, and join a Martian band. They wind up playing at halftime in the Super Bowl, where they're *flush*ed with excitement.

Next there's a movie about a mad scientist, *Dr. Midas*. Everything he touches turns to gold, so he runs for president, shakes a lot of hands, and becomes very rich. Unfortunately, he makes a bad investment when he picks his nose.

After that, there's another movie called *Eggs-tra Terrestrial*, about a hen-pecked husband who creates a giant chicken. Right before he takes over the world, he drowns in a large omelette. The police suspect *fowl* play.

Next there's *The Brainiac,* about a guy who turns ants into *gi*-ants. It's no picnic for him when they eat him out of house and home . . . and then eat him. He should have turned them into uncles.

Mom grabs the remote and beams me up to bed. If I only had my clone . . .

CHAPTER 6
BUS BUSTLE

BLAW!
BLAW!
BLAW!

The next morning on the school bus, all the kids are talking about their science projects. Eric's down because he couldn't come up with one body part. No one lifted a *finger* to help him.

223

I can still see Derek, so he's not doing so well. Doris isn't talking much about her colossal invention. But Freddy says that he's making progress. He's one whole day into the future since yesterday.

Penny is still working on her telescope — with no end in sight. I tell her to get a movie magazine, where she's sure to see lots of stars. Randy's still trying to get his project off the ground.

WHICH END DO YOU LOOK THROUGH?

DAD'S LEAF BLOWER DOESN'T GIVE ME ENOUGH BOOST FOR BLAST OFF.

And I'm still undecided. It's between cloning myself and making a laugh machine. It's down to cloning or clowning!

CHAPTER 7
A BLAST FROM THE PAST

THE LIBRARIAN

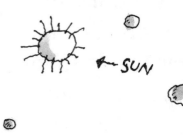

← SUN

○ ← ONLY A CIRCLE

GALLEYOYO

In the library, Mrs. Beamster tells us about great scientists from the past. A guy named *Galleyoyo* said the earth was not the center of the universe. He made a lot of self-centered people mad.

EARTH →

☾ ← MOON

227

When Christopher Columbus said the earth was round, a lot of squares gave him a hard time.

Another guy named *Listermint*, made people angry when he told them to wash their hands to kill germs. I think that he was in *Germ*any. And a scientist named *Pasture* washed milk to get rid of *paris*ites. I think that he was from Paris.

GERMS

HOLD UP YOUR ARMS PLEASE.

228

Another scientist named Newton was hit by a fig and invented the Fig Newton. *Ben Frankly* was shocked when everyone told him to go fly a kite. And Alexander Graham Bell invented graham crackers for your *belly*.

Mrs. Beamster says that everything we have today came from someone's imagination. And all the things we'll have tomorrow will come from ours. Boy, am I pumped!

CARS WITHOUT WHEELS.

YOUR VERY OWN WALKING AIR CONDITIONER.

HI, MOM.

A TOOTH PHONE YOU ALWAYS HAVE IN YOUR MOUTH.

EXACT SIZE.

ACHOO!

A PILL TO CURE THE COMMON COLD.

CHAPTER 8
THE NAME GAME

I'm so excited! I check out a book called *How Inventions and Other Things Got Their Names.* It's very interesting. For instance, the guy who first ate an artichoke was named *Arty* and he *choked.*

CHAPTER 9
TOO MANY ME'S

(CLONING) (LAUGH MACHINE)

WHICH SCIENCE PROJECT DO YOU THINK HUBIE SHOULD DO?

☆ CHOOSE ONE→

On the school bus ride home, I still can't decide whether I should clone myself or build a laugh machine. While I look out the bus window, I start to daydream about the science fair. But it's more like a *day-mare*!

I'm running on the playground. It's a bright, sunny day. I'm feeling good, but all of a sudden I bump into me.

"Why don't you look where I'm going?" I ask.

"Why don't you?" I reply.

We begin to argue, and a third me comes over to settle the fight, but he agrees with both of us. So we call over a fourth me. He's no help, either, and soon we're surrounded by a crowd of me's.

I ask, "Why don't we go play basketball?" But I can't seem to agree with myself.

Eleven me's want to play baseball, and I just want to wake up!

Suddenly, the bus horn honks and all the other me's vanish. I wipe my brow and decide not to clone myself. I look back into the window for a second opinion, but luckily I agree with me.

CHAPTER 10
GENIUS AT WORK

When I get off the bus, I go straight home from school and get to work. I realize that if I cloned myself, I would have to share my allowance. Bummer!

THANKS FOR THE DOLLAR.

DRAT.

CHUCKLE!
CHUCKLE!
CHUCKLE!

DAD'S SHAVING CREAM

So I'm going for the laugh machine. I mess up my hair, put on my crazy eyeball glasses, my white *laugh* coat, and go into my *laugh*ratory.

Maybe I'll just begin with a giggle machine or a chuckle box and work my way up. I squirt my dad's shaving cream on top of my head. I rub my mom's lipstick on the end of my nose. I look in the mirror and chuckle.

GIGGLE BOX

239

But when I go outside and show my dog, Tailspin, he just runs and hides. I show my mom, and she just tells me to go wash my face for dinner. Oh, well, back to the drawing board!

HUBIE, TIME FOR DINNER.

HOW DO I LOOK, MOM?

CHAPTER 11

A TOUGH ROW TO HO!

After dinner, I work late into the night. At 9:30 p.m., Mom tells me to go to bed. I still don't have my laugh machine finished, and tomorrow is the science fair.

When I fall asleep that night, I have a scream dream. It's the day of the fair. All the kids are in the gym with their projects.

Eric's monster is ten feet tall and sewn together. It looks like a cross between Coach Kong and Mrs. Beamster. It has a bolt in its neck and an outlet for its belly button. Eric tells it jokes to keep it in stitches.

I don't see Derek, but I guess that's a good sign. Doris's project is covered with a blanket and labeled TOP SECRET!

Penny's telescope looks like the one at the planetarium. I bet her father helped her. Randy's climbing aboard his rocket. And Freddy pulls the lever on his time machine. There's a *pop, bop,* and *boom!* When the smoke clears, we're all standing in the future.

Freddy has a beard and is old enough to drive, but there are no more cars. In fact, there are no more streets, just sidewalks everywhere. Bummer!

There was just too much pollution, so now everyone has to walk. There's a walk-through fast-food place, a walk-by bank, and walk-in movie theaters. Even NASCAR is *NASWALK*.

Freddy is sad. I guess now it's

time for my laugh machine. I wind it up and it says, "Ho, ho, ho!" But no one else is laughing. They all just walk away.

I wake up and roll out of bed. It's Saturday—time for the science fair.

CHAPTER 12
BRAINSTORM!

While I'm brushing my teeth, I suddenly have it! Yes! It will work. I high-five the mirror and get to work.

LUNCH!

By 11:00 a.m., I'm putting on the finishing touches. I print LAUGH MACHINE on my T-shirt. The science fair is at 1:00 p.m. I put on my backpack and I'm ready to roll.

I sit in the van and feel like I'm driving into the future. If I win first prize at the science fair, I'll go on to become a famous *fizzy*-cist and invent lots of neat stuff.

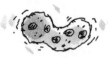

And my best invention will be my *Lazy-ier Ray.* When people get excited and want to fight, I'll zap them with my *Lazy-ier Ray* and they'll just yawn and go back to bed. I'll call it the *Have-A-Nice-Day Ray* and I will win the *No Bell Pizza Prize.*

We pull up at school. I get out of the van and walk into the gym with confidence.

CHAPTER 13
OUR INVENTION CONVENTION

All the kids are standing by their projects. There are lots of cool things to see. I hope people like my laugh machine.

Instead of Frankenstein, Eric brought in his dog, Butch, who has a bolt in his collar.

ANSWER: (A)

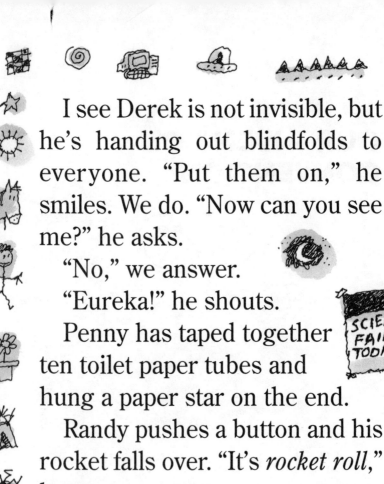

I see Derek is not invisible, but he's handing out blindfolds to everyone. "Put them on," he smiles. We do. "Now can you see me?" he asks.

"No," we answer.

"Eureka!" he shouts.

Penny has taped together ten toilet paper tubes and hung a paper star on the end.

Randy pushes a button and his rocket falls over. "It's *rocket roll*," he says.

Freddy has a sign that his time machine is in the future and won't be back until tomorrow.

And Doris still isn't showing her project to anybody.

ANSWER: (A)

I guess it's time for my laugh machine. I turn around and open my backpack. I put on my googly eyes, my vampire fangs, my picnic plate ears, and my propeller beanie. I twirl my propeller, stick my finger in my nose, spin around three times, cross my eyes, press my belly button and . . . burp!

252

Everyone laughs, even Mrs. Green. She awards me a special prize for the "Silliest Invention."

Hey, science is a blast! Maybe next year we'll have our science fair on the moon, and I'll be an astro-*nut!*

THE
HALLOWEEN PARTY
FROM THE
BLACK LAGOON

To Tom and Suzanne
—M.T.

In memory of:
Eddie Stanley, Jr.
February 21, 1998

My best buddy ever.
—J.L.

CHAPTER 1
HALLO-WHEN?

Mrs. Green says that we're going to have a Halloween party at school. Next *Fright-day*, we all have to come to class in costumes. Then we'll all vote and pick the best one. Mrs. Green says there's a totally awesome first prize.

I have no idea who or what I should come as. Maybe I should just stay home that day and come as the Invisible Man.

ARF
ARF
ARF

CHAPTER 2
DISGUISE THE LIMIT

On the school bus, all the kids are excited about their costumes. Eric says he has a beautiful rubber mask. The eyeball is hanging out and there's an ax stuck in the brain. Needless to say, there's lots of fake blood on it.

THIS IS SO COOL.

The girls are not impressed. Penny says there's an ax stuck in Eric's brain all the time, and that she may come as a princess. Eric says he'll be happy to crown her.

PLEASE BOW.

Doris waves her arm and says that she's coming as a ballet dancer. The boys are not at all impressed.

Freddy is coming as a werewolf—claws and all. Eric says he should come as an *underwear-wolf.* Randy is coming as Count Dracula. He says it's a disguise you can really sink your teeth into.

IM A SWAN.

WEIRDWOLF

BURP.

FULL MOON

UNDERWEAR-WOLF

WHAT IS DRACULA'S FAVORITE FRUIT?

ANSWER ON PAGE 274.

263

And Derek is coming as a mummy.

Eric says, "Why not come as a daddy? And what about you, Hubie?"

"Me . . . oh, my costume's still in the planning stage," I reply. The truth is, I have no idea what I will come as. I'm having an identity crisis!

I'M ALL WRAPPED UP IN MY COSTUME.

CHAPTER 3
GO FOR BROKE!

When I get home, I empty my piggy bank, but there's not a lot in it. I'm able to shake out $2.38. This is not good.

I don't have high hopes as I get on my bike and pedal toward the costume shop. When I arrive, it's monster mayhem!

Every aisle is fiend-filled.
Blood and guts galore. It's like
going to the movies. Every
major monster is there—
Frankenstein, Dracula, Wolfman,
and the Thing. It's all fur, fangs,
blood, and bolts.

Everything looks really cool. The only problem is the price tags are monstrous, too. There's nothing less than thirty dollars. Even the masks are all more than ten dollars. I recount my money. It's not $2.38. It's $2.37.

← SCAR   ← WORM

NOODLE →

The saleswoman isn't very helpful. She just says to go look on the sale rack by the door. Well, there's a scar for $2.99, an eyeball for $3.99, a set of fangs for $4.99, and a tube that squirts fake blood for $5.99.

I open my hand and look at my $2.37. I can afford one Martian antenna or one witch's wart, but that's not going to make a great costume. I'm going to have to look elsewhere.

OPEN

THE MONSTER COSTUME SHOP
AND CAFE

ENTER AT YOUR OWN RISK →

BRAINS FOR SALE

KING KONG

268

← SPIDERS

← SNAKE

CHAPTER 4
A HOME REMEDY

As I slouch on the couch, Mom comes over and sits down next to me. "What's the matter?" she asks.

I tell her about the Halloween party, the contest, and my costume problem. She smiles, takes my hand, and leads me up to the attic. There she opens an old trunk and pulls out a cardboard crown.

ATTIC

271

"When I was a little girl, we didn't have much money either," she smiles while putting on the crown. "So I just made my own costumes, like this princess costume." She straightens two of the crown's droopy points.

"That's a great idea, Mom," I say as she looks in the mirror.

WHAT DO YOU CALL A MONSTER WHO HAS A BABY?
ANSWER: PAGE 281.

She skipped back to the trunk and pulled out a big pink eraser cap. "Another year, I was a number two pencil," she winks while putting on the cap. "It was a pretty *sharp* costume."

"I get the *point*, Mom, but I don't know *what* to be," I sigh.

"Just use your imagination, Hubie." She smiles, pats me on the shoulder, and goes back downstairs as an eraser head.

A DINER-SAUR

EAT

OPEN

ANSWER: A NECK-TARINE

275

CHAPTER 5
A SCREAM OF A DREAM

That night, I have one crazy dream. I'm at school, but my whole class is full of monsters . . . *real* monsters! They all have a hard time fitting into their desks, especially the Blob.

Finally, they get settled down, and Mrs. Green calls the roll.

Frankenstein raises his hand and it falls off.

"I'm here, here, and here," says the Blob.

And Dracula pulls the witch's hair, so she turns him into a bloodhound.

I just sit there as quiet as can be. "We're going to have a party for Halloween," says Mrs. Green. All of the monsters start fidgeting in their desks. They're all worried about their costumes. Frankenstein says he may come as Elvis.

Dracula thinks he may be a nurse from the blood bank. And the Wolfman may dress up as a schnauzer.

I tell the witch that she could be a pencil, and the Blob that he could be a Brussels sprout. They all look at me. "And what are you going to be, Hubie?" they all ask.

Luckily, I wake up before I have to answer them. I just stare up at the ceiling. I don't even see the distant glimmer of an idea. I think my imagination still must be sleeping.

FOOD FOR THOUGHT

HOW TO BE CREATIVE

IDEAS THAT WORK

CHAPTER 6
CLOTHES ENCOUNTERS

← MRS. BEAMSTER, THE LIBRARIAN.

The next day, I go to the library in search of inspiration. Mrs. Beamster gives me a book on costumes.

Boy, people sure used to dress funny. They didn't always wear baseball caps and sneakers. They wore tunics, tights, sandals, and bedsheets!

281

·ANSWER: A MOMSTER

I wonder if in a hundred years our clothes will look as funny to future folks.

Mrs. Beamster says that in other parts of the world, even today, people dress differently than we do.

I could wear my bathrobe and be a sheik, or I could be Santa Claus, or even a submarine. Whoa, now my imagination has finally woken up—I'm on my way!

KING HUBIE

HUBIE CLAUS

HO HO HO

DIVE! DIVE!

ARF ARF

HU-BOAT

SUB

PASS THE MUSTARD.

CHAPTER 7
THE PICK OF
THE GLITTER

Well, now the problem is I have too many ideas! I could make a big bun out of pillows and be a hot dog. Maybe I could put a pillow on my head and be a marshmallow.

I could draw a dial on my belly and be a cell phone. I could even cut a window in a box, draw a keyboard, and be a computer. Or I could get between two pieces of cardboard and be a book. There's so much to be!

285

On my way home from school, all the possibilities are parading in my mind. Then we pass a billboard with an angel on it. Hmmm, an angel? That's it! I'll be an angel. I'm on cloud nine.

GOLD
PAINT
(SHAKE
WELL)

CHAPTER 8
WINGING IT!

At home, I get to work. I take a wire coat hanger and bend it into a halo. It's easy—a little circle on top and a bigger circle on the bottom that fits on my head. It looks a little like a TV antenna, so I spray it with gold paint.

COAT HANGER (WIRE NOT WOOD)

PLIERS
(ASK MOM
FOR HELP)

MAKING A
HALO
WHAT YOU NEED

COOL

Wings—how am I going to make those? Two pillows don't work. Two paper plates look lame. Mom says to get some cardboard and she'll help me cut out wings. Mom is a good artist. She draws me a pair of wings. Then I cut them out, but they still look like they are made of cardboard.

WINGS

PILLOWS- **NO!**

GLOVES- **NO!**

PAPER PLATES- **NO!**

TENNIS RACKETS- **NO!**

PLASTIC MILK BOTTLES- **NO!**

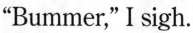

"Bummer," I sigh.

Suddenly, out of nowhere, Mom yells out, "Feathers! We need lots of feathers."

We both look at Peeper, our parakeet. No-ooo way! Peeper needs all the feathers he's got.

"Hmmm. Let's try the park," says Mom.

We drive over, but the pigeons want to keep all theirs, too.

So we rush over to the market. But we're out of *pluck*. All the chickens are already naked.

"Pillows!" shouts Mom. "What was I thinking?! Pillows are full of feathers. And we have lots of those at home."

We speed home and find an old down pillow. Mom opens it up and shakes it out. Now we are in fine feather weather.

Feathers float and fall all over the room like snowflakes.

Mom and I catch them in midair and glue them to the wings. Now they look like they belong to an angel. I'm almost ready to fly!

THANKS, MOM.

PILLOW ↓

GLUE

CHAPTER 9
THE BIG DAY!

It's Friday morning, and it's the big day—Halloween party time! I am so excited I can't stop moving.

I start to get ready. I put on a white T-shirt and my white bathing suit. Mom puts my wings on my back with duct tape. Easy as pie!

I put on my halo and look in the mirror. There was even some cardboard left over and I made a little cloud. I look cool—simply heavenly.

CLOUD NINE →

CHAPTER 10
HALLOWEEN SCENE

When the school bus pulls up, it looks like it just came from the cemetery. Eric's eyeball is swinging back and forth. And instead of a hat . . . he's wearing a *hat-chet*! Gross!

Freddy's got on rubber claws, and he's trying to pick his nose. Even more gross!

Penny decided to be a witch. I recognize her $1.99 wart. She's casting spells on Derek to turn him into a frog. But he's wrapped in toilet paper and already beginning to unwind.

ERIC

FREDDY

PENNY

DEREK

295

Randy is Count Dracula. He's got the $4.99 fangs and a cape. Doris is dressed in her tutu and ballet shoes. She looks a lot like a dancer.

I have to stand up all the way to school because I don't want to bend my wings.

YOU CAN COUNT ON ME.

I'M TUTU COOL.

RANDY

DORIS

BAT

CHAPTER 11
PARTY ANIMALS

Mrs. Green has done an awesome job decorating our classroom. It looks like a real swamp.

There are big black spiders with crepe paper legs—wiggling on the walls. Jack-o'-lanterns with candles are glowing in the corner. And striped snakes made from toilet paper tubes are rolling around on the floor.

There are lots of funny signs like: LOOK OUT FOR ALLIGATORS!; WELCOME GHASTLY GHOSTS AND GRUESOME GHOULS FROM GRISLY GRAVES!; and CREEPY CRAWLING CROSSING!

Mrs. Green is in a cool costume, too. She's dressed like a baseball player. She has a uniform, a cap, and a bat.

We all sit at our desks and she takes attendance. "Wolfman?"

"Here," says Freddy, raising his paw.

"Mr. Eyeball Hatchet Head?"

"Here," says Eric, swinging his orb.

Mrs. Green continues to do the roll call.

"Count Dracula?"

"Heeeere," shouts Randy, as he chomps his fangs.

"Miss Witch?"

"I'm here," squeals Penny, wiggling her fingers.

"Mummy?"

"Here," moans Derek, still unwinding down the aisle.

"Prima Ballerina?"

"Here," sings Doris, raising her arm to look like a swan.

"And our Angel?"

"Here," I say, trying to flap my wings.

Big mistake. A flutter of feathers fills the room.

"Well, we're all here," says Mrs. Green as she closes her attendance book. "And how wonderful you all look."

Eric swivels his eyeball around to survey the room. "Now, let's have our contest. Come up front, one at a time, and tell us a little about your costume. Penny, you'll be first," says Mrs. Green, pointing her bat.

← INVISIBLE BOY

BATBOY ←

CHAPTER 12
SHARING WHAT YOU'RE WEARING

Penny sails up on a broom to the front of the class. "I'm a witch, and you're all going to be frogs," she says, wiggling her fingers.

"Which witch are you?" shouts Derek.

"I'm the *sand-witch* in the kitchen," proclaims Penny as she floats back to her seat.

Derek's next. He unwinds all the way up to the front. "I'm a mummy, and I'm two thousand years old."

"You don't look a day over one thousand," yells Eric.

"Watch what you're saying, Eric," says Mrs. Green.

Eric puts his dangling eyeball into his mouth.

I'M A COOL GHOUL.

"I live in a state of *deNile*," smiles Derek.

"Time to wrap it up," says Mrs. Green.

"Okay. Knock, knock," says Derek.

"Who's there?" asks everyone.

"Mummified," smiles Derek.

"Mummified who?" we ask.

"My mummified me a yummy hamburger for lunch today," laughs Derek.

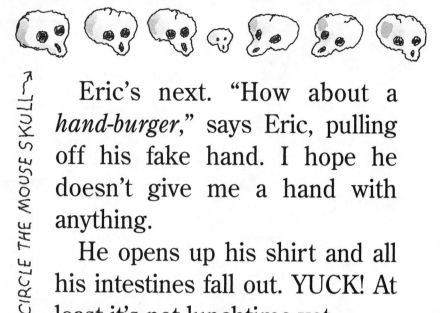

Eric's next. "How about a *hand-burger*," says Eric, pulling off his fake hand. I hope he doesn't give me a hand with anything.

He opens up his shirt and all his intestines fall out. YUCK! At least it's not lunchtime yet.

"You've certainly got a lot of guts," smiles Mrs. Green. I love when teachers make jokes.

Soon Doris spins down the aisle, twirls, and bows.

CLAP CLAP CLAP CLAP

309

Then Freddy bounds up and raises his paws. "A poem," he starts to recite. "Does a werewolf wear underwear underneath all his hair?"

"I'm unaware, but I am next," I answer as I fly up front in a flurry of feathers. And I almost lose my halo.

"I'm an angel," I smile, straightening my halo.

"Just remember that for the rest of the year," smiles Mrs. Green. I hate it when teachers make jokes.

Randy's last. He slinks up front. "Allow me to *entrodouth* myself. I am Count Dracula from Transylvania."

"You need a *Transyl-fusion*," shouts Eric.

"Eric, please pull yourself together," says Mrs. Green.

"I'm a little batty," continues Randy as he holds up his cape and flaps back to his seat.

"Well, you all look beautiful," says Mrs. Green. "But we have to pick a winner for the grand prize."

VERY NICE, KIDS.

WHAT IS DRACULA'S FAVORITE HOLIDAY?

ANSWER: PAGE 314

313

"What *is* the grand prize?" asks Eric, snapping his eyeball.

"The grand prize is a $35 gift certificate to the costume shop," says Mrs. Green, twirling her bat.

After a lot of "oohs" and "ahs," the class votes. It's really close because all my classmates vote for themselves.

THE WINNER IS...

AWESOME

OOH

AH

COOL

GIFT CERTIFICATE

VOTES

314

But do you know who wins? I do.

I have two votes. Someone else voted for me. As I look around the room, Eric winks his eyeball.

What a buddy! I'm going to share the grand prize with him. I'll get him a rubber heart that he can wear on his sleeve.

315

CIRCLE THE BOWLING BALL

As for me, I've got everything I want. Angels don't need much. Well, maybe I'll just get a little harp.

THE
FIELD DAY
FROM THE
BLACK LAGOON

3-LEGGED RACE

To Jan and Sylvia,
true brother and sister
open hearts — open arms
—M.T.

To my best man,
Larry Fasse
—J.L.

← COACH KONG.

CHAPTER 1
THE AGONY OF DA-FEET

Coach Kong marches us into the gym and lines us up. He paces back and forth, holding his clipboard. "Next Friday, we're having a field day," he declares.

He reads off some of the events from his list. I nervously start picking at the rubber on my sneakers. It sounds like the script for an action movie.

"Parachute," says Coach Kong.

Do we have to jump out of an airplane?

320

GET THE LEAD OUT!

EVENTS
1. ꙮꙮꙮꙮꙮ
2. ꙮꙮ ꙮꙮꙮ
3. ꙮꙮꙮꙮ
4. ꙮꙮ

"Obstacle course," he continues.
Do we have to run through fire, leap over lions, hop over hippos, skip through snakes, and tiptoe around tigers?

321

Then there's Charlie Over the
Water. They fill a big tank with
hungry sharks and throw us in.
That gets you ready for the One-
Legged Race.

I don't think I *field* so good. I
ask Coach Kong if everyone has
to be at the field day. He just
laughs and says, "It'll be a day
you'll never forget."

CHAPTER 2
LAUNCH TIME

At lunch, we eat big bean burritos and look over the stuff to do at next Friday's field day event. There's the Bean Bag Toss. That should be easy—we just ate 'em.

There's another event called Scarf Tag. Eric says they should make an event called Barf Tag because it would be so cool and gross. Some of the girls move to another table. It's so easy to make them queasy!

BARF BAG
(KEEP COOL)

← THIS SIDE UP.

We read off another one, Three-Legged Race—that should require major surgery. OUCH!

Then there's the Tug-of-War. This is going to be survival of the fittest. I don't fit at all.

STATION 1

STATION 2

324

Who knows? Maybe I'll win the Sack Race. I am a good sleeper.

Penny and Doris say that they will luck out and win a bunch of events like Jump Rope, Hula-Hoop, and Egg Race.

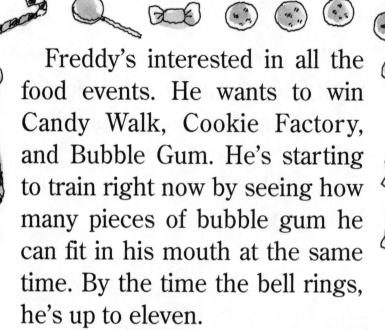

Freddy's interested in all the food events. He wants to win Candy Walk, Cookie Factory, and Bubble Gum. He's starting to train right now by seeing how many pieces of bubble gum he can fit in his mouth at the same time. By the time the bell rings, he's up to eleven.

I LOVE THIS EVENT.

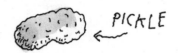
PICKLE ←

CHAPTER 3
OLYM-PICKLES

On the way home, all the kids are talking about the field day. Freddy says it's just like the Olympics. That's right, I think—we'll all *limp* home.

"I'm a good jumper," brags Derek.

"I'm a good bumper," blurts Freddy.

"I'm fast," declares Randy.

"I'm last," I sigh.

OOPS!

For the rest of the way home, Eric and I discuss the situation. There's not going to be even one video game—bummer! So we're going to have to get into shape.

But what shape should we get into? Square, round, triangular? Eric says, "Muscles . . . we need muscles . . . FAST!"

"What about clams?" I ask. "Do we need clams, too?"

He rolls his eyes and says, "We have to get fit, Hubie."

"To fit what?" I ask.

Eric says that he's going to get fit, and I should shape up. It's all too confusing. I just stare out the window and count red convertibles.

THERE'S ONE.

SCHOOL BUS

RED

CHAPTER 4
MUSCLE-BOUND

When I get home, I realize Eric had a point, and it wasn't just the top of his head. I need some muscles . . . quick, if I want to win any events.

330

I EAT MUSCLES.

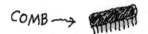 

On TV that night, there's an ad for muscles. It's a complete body-building system for $19.95. Normally, it sells for $385. But if you call in the next five minutes, they'll cut the price in half to $9.97.

It's called Wimpflex and it guarantees muscles in eight days or your money back.

The field day is in six days. Maybe I could go from total wimp to almost wonderful. I check my piggy bank. I have ten dollars—I'm on my way—I call in. Look out, field day, here I come!

BANK

I HAVE TEN DOLLARS IN COINS.

←—SHRIMP

I send off my money and wait. Every day I check the mailbox after school. Days pass. I'm getting weaker and weaker. Then three days later, it comes!

My complete Wimpflex body-building system. I eagerly open the little box. It's a rubber band and a booklet. Well, I read the booklet and start right away to make up for lost time. Maybe I can go from shrimp to strong-man before the field day.

ANYTHING FOR ME?

AND ME?

333

CHAPTER 5
MY PER-PLEX MACHINE

The first exercise is for abs. What's an ab?

It says, "Lie down." That's easy. I can do that. Then it says, "Sit up." I just lay down and got comfortable, why would I sit up?

STEP1

STEP 2

STEP 3

REPEAT STEP 1

BICEPS

ABS

I move on to the next section. It says, "Biceps." Do I have to buy something else? There's a picture of an arm. Okay, it says, "Put your Wimpflex around a door handle and pull." It's a silly way to open the door, but I'll try it. While I'm pulling, Mom opens the door, and my rubber band snaps. I go flying across the room.

Well, so much for biceps. Maybe I won't need 'em for field day.

SNAP!

WIMP

The next exercise is for pecs, and the one after that is for thighs. I think this is a body-building system for chickens. I want my money back.

I phone the number on the booklet. A man answers. I tell him that I'm not satisfied. He says that my Wimpflex is

SUPER CHICKEN

PECS

THIGHS

guaranteed to give me muscles. Then he asks if I'm holding up the phone.

I say, "Yes."

He says that if I'm holding the phone, I have muscles, and then I hear a click. I look at my $9.97 rubber band and start to feel sad. I just got conned!

CHAPTER 6
A HEALTHY ATTITUDE

The next day, Mom tells me that walking is the best exercise. I can walk, so I am in good shape.

She also says that a well-balanced diet is important.

She claims, "You are what you eat."

So I ask for a hot dog. I'd like to be a hot dog at the field day.

HOT DOG

COLD DOG

Later that day, I go to the health food store. The shelves are loaded with products and promises. Power Powder says that it can give you a healthier body in three days. Another is called Energizer—I don't want to eat a battery, though. There is even some stuff called Muscle Maker and another thing called Puny Pills. I don't think I want any of them.

GRRRRRR

CATTAILS

339

I walk farther into the store and there's row after row of powders, pills, and potions that all say they are packed with power.

Each one promises a healthier body in three minutes or three days.

There are Brawn Bars, Force Flakes, and Tower Tabs that strengthen, invigorate, and fortify.

IF YOU TAKE ONE OF THESE A DAY YOU'LL LOOK LIKE ME.

COOL.

POWER GUY PRODUCTS

POWER GUY

There's another product called Lightning Bar—one bite will turn you into an Olympic champion and two bites will give you the power to fly. I don't think there's a flying competition at the field day.

Another aisle contains a whole alphabet of vitamins and minerals. And all the store's signs say that you need to buy them all.

AWESOME.

Then there's a weird food area. Hot dogs made from cereal. Cereal made from seaweed. Then there's tofu, which sounds like it comes from in between your toes. GROSS! And it's all really, really expensive.

I wonder if they'd like to buy my rubber band.

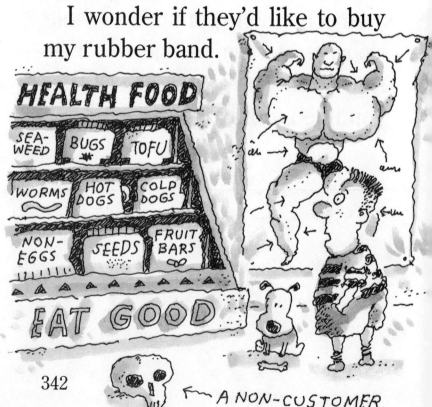

HEALTH FOOD

SEA-WEED | BUGS | TOFU

WORMS | HOT DOGS | COLD DOGS

NON-EGGS | SEEDS | FRUIT BARS

EAT GOOD

A NON-CUSTOMER

CHAPTER 7
PICK ON ME!

THEY DIDN'T NOTICE MY PECS.

I'm in training. I mean I played with my electric train for hours. Nobody at school notices my new muscles, but I know they're under my shirt somewhere.

Coach Kong says it's time to choose teams for tomorrow's field day.

DOLLAR ⟶   ⟵ BAD FOR FLIPPING.

Eric and Derek are the captains. We all line up and they flip a coin to see who goes first. Eric wins and picks Freddy, who now can get twenty-six pieces of bubble gum into his mouth. I flex my bicep, but Derek picks Randy because he's the fastest kid in class. Then I flex my abs, and Eric picks me because he's my best friend.

ANCHOR→

That just leaves Doris and Penny. Doris weighs more than Penny, so we could use her as an anchor for our team. Well, Derek picks her, and Penny joins our team. She's very thin. Maybe we could use her as a rope--that might be helpful!

COACH KONG

345

I wish Superman or The Hulk was on our team. Oh well, we'll have to do our best without them.

After school, I ride my bike to a local gym. Standing by the door, I watch other people work out. Boy, they sweat a lot. They smell, too! YUCK!

346

Then I ride over to the health food store and breathe in the air. I hope some of it will make me healthier and stronger.

I'm doing everything I can do to get into shape.

I even read my Wimpflex booklet over again. I hope that is some sort of exercise. Afterward, I watch a bodybuilding movie and pray that my muscles can see how rock-hard they should be. I hope that I am ready for tomorrow.

LET ME GIVE YOU A HAND.

COOL.

CHAPTER 8
DOOM AND GLOOM

Later that night, I have a nightmare—well, it's more like a field-mare. YIKES!

It's tomorrow, and the field day has started. . . .

Derek, Randy, and Doris have all grown into ten-foot-tall giants. Coach Kong has joined their team as well. They even have team uniforms and a team name—THE GIANTS.

← NIGHTMARE

Eric, Freddy, Penny, and I are called the Wimps. Boy, I wish I had my rubber band.

The first event is the Tug-of-War. Our team holds on tightly to the rope. The Giants give one yank and we go sailing over the school!

The next event is the Soccer Kick. They kick us instead of the ball. And we go sailing over the school again!

After that, the Bean Bag Toss starts. But the Giants toss us. Once again, we go sailing over the school.

The last event is Bubble Gum Blowout. Freddy is now able to get 240 pieces of bubble gum into his mouth.

Then he blows a gigantic
bubble. It gets bigger and
bigger. He begins to float up.

We grab on to him and together
we all sail over the school. Our
team is disqualified for leaving
the playing field.

 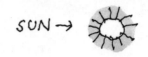

I wake up and I've fallen out of bed . . . right into Friday. It's time for the field day! Hope our team's ready.

354

CHAPTER 9
LET THE GAMES BEGIN

On the bus to school, everyone is bragging. My team and Derek's team are both bursting with boasts and insults:

"We're better . . . you're butter," they yell.

"Oh yeah, we're champs," we reply. "You're chumps."

BUTTER

 BUTTERFLY

WINNER → (boy: THANK YOU.)

WHINER → (girl: I WAS TRIPPED.)

"Oh yeah, we're winners," they reply. "You're whiners."

Wow, that one kind of stung.

"Whatever, we're number one and you're done," our team yells out.

"All of you cut that out," says Mr. Fenderbender, the school bus driver. "It's not whether you win or lose . . . It's how you play the game."

"That's right," says Eric. "And we'll play it better than Derek's team."

"I don't think so," says Derek. "Because we're going to crush you. Then mush you. And afterward turn you into slush!"

The funny thing is, we were all good friends yesterday, before we chose teams.

CHAPTER 10
FIELD OF BATTLE

Well, we survive the trip to school, but now no one's talking to one another. We're all finely tuned athletes focused on the challenges that lie before us. I feel like we're at the Olympic Games, marching out onto the field of battle.

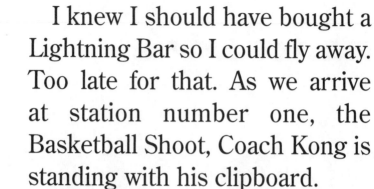

I knew I should have bought a Lightning Bar so I could fly away. Too late for that. As we arrive at station number one, the Basketball Shoot, Coach Kong is standing with his clipboard.

"Okay," he says. "What are the team names?"

Derek shouts out, "The Tigers!"

Coach writes it down and turns to us.

STATION 1
BASKETBALL SHOOT

361

Oh my gosh, Eric and I didn't know that we had to have a team name. We both look at each other.

Then Penny shouts out, "The Pussycats."

Coach Kong writes it down.

"Meow," snickers Derek.

"This could be cat-astrophic," shouts Eric.

Then Coach Kong gives out the basketballs. He hands one to

MEOW.

Penny. She's our best free throw shooter. Sure enough, she sinks all of her baskets.

Derek doesn't get any in and misses the backboard completely. We win the event and we put our best paw forward.

Station number two is the Three-Legged Race. Coach ties my leg to Eric's and then ties Derek's to Randy's. Then he yells, "On your mark, get set, go!"

We're off and hobbling. I don't know how spiders walk with eight legs. Our legs get tangled, and we fall over. It's obvious Derek and Randy have been practicing, because they win by two noses.

DIRECTIONS

① CHOOSE SOMEBODY YOU LIKE.

② TIE YOUR MIDDLE LEGS TOGETHER.

③ PUT YOUR LEFT ARM AROUND YOUR PARTNER.

④ TOGETHER, MOVE YOUR LEFT LEG FORWARD, THEN YOUR RIGHT.

⑤ REPEAT UNTIL YOU CROSS THE FINISH LINE.

ROPE

THE THREE-LEGGED RACE

We're tied, one to one. Next is the Water Balloon Toss, and Derek's team drowns. They lose with a big splash! Our team floats to the top with a win.

We're ahead two to one, but then they catch up in the Ring Toss. Randy is a ringer. I didn't know he was so good. But we pull ahead with a Hula-Hoop victory. Penny out-wiggles Doris. She's really hip!

EASY PICKINGS.

YEAH, BABY!

SHE'S TOO GOOD.

The Tigers catch up in the Bean Bag Toss. And we have our first casualty. Eric gets beaned with a bag and has to go see Miss Hearse. Derek calls Eric a beanie baby as he leaves the field.

After a few minutes, Eric's back out on the field in a flash. He's hopping mad for the Sack Race. We bounce back into the lead by sacking them with a win.

I'LL SHOW THEM WHO'S THE BABY!

YEAH!

HOP
HOP
HOP
HOP

FINISH

TIGER →

But then the Tigers give us the boot and win the Soccer Kick contest. Now we're all tied up again going into the Bubble Gum blowout.

CHAPTER 11
A BLOWOUT

Our hopes are riding on Freddy, who can now get twenty-nine pieces of bubble gum into his mouth. Eric and I keep shoving it in until his cheeks are puffed out like softballs.

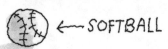 ←—SOFTBALL

371

When he tries to blow, Freddy just starts turning an odd shade of blue and we have to rush him to Miss Hearse, who does an emergency extraction with pliers. Derek's team wins the event, and our whole team is blue.

STAY BACK. GIVE HIM SOME AIR.

MY HAND IS STUCK!

NURSE, WILL HE BE OK?

HE'LL BE FINE.

HAT→ ←CAKE

But we rally and take the Cake Walk.

EASY!

THAT WAS CLOSE.

DON'T STEP ON THE CAKES.

It's tied again! Now it's all riding on the last event—the Tug-of-War. Can we pull it off?

Freddy, who still is a shade of aqua, is our anchor. The Tigers' anchor is Doris. She looks pretty tough. We line up on the rope and spit on our hands. We're off!

WALK. DON'T RUN.

We huff and puff. We tug and chug. We yank and crank. We heave and haul, but nobody's budging at all—not even an inch!

374

IF 15 MINUTES HAVE PAST, HOW MANY MINUTES ARE LEFT IN AN HOUR? ANSWER ON PAGE 378.

TICK TICK TICK

After fifteen minutes of major exertion, Coach Kong blows his whistle, and he declares the field day a tie. We let go of the rope and all fall down laughing and rolling around. Everyone's beat, but a winner!

CHAPTER 12
HAPPY ENDING

So we all get to celebrate because we're all field day champs. As a reward, each of us gets a Popsicle and a gold medal. Well, not really gold, more like yellow cardboard medals made by Miss Swamp.

MISS SWAMP, THE ART TEACHER.

But we wear our medals with pride on the bus ride home and talk all about what a great time we had at the field day.

The field day totally rocked! Then we all laugh together, remembering all the fun stuff that had nothing to do with winning, like the water balloons bursting and the look on Freddy's face when he tried to blow a bubble.

When I get home, I find my rubber band and throw it in the trash. I don't need a gimmick to be a winner!

Maybe next year for the field day, I'll start exercising more and be as big as Mr. Universe. Well, maybe that's stretching it a little. At least I know that it'll be a field day of fun.

HUBIE NEXT YEAR... (MAYBE).

STAR

378

THE
SCHOOL CARNIVAL
FROM THE
BLACK LAGOON

For little Laurel Dillon,
Welcome to the world!
—M.T.

To Kent and Jon, two clowns
—J.L.

CHAPTER 1
A BOOTH, FOR SOOTH

Our school is having a carnival. Mrs. Green says that our class has to run a booth. But what kind will it be?

She says it has to be lots of fun, easy to run, and make a ton of money! If we raise enough, we can have a real, live author come to our school. If we don't, maybe we could afford a not-so-alive author.

COOL.

SCHOOL
CARNIVAL

383

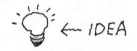 ← IDEA

Mrs. Green wants each of us to bring an idea for a carnival booth tomorrow. It is our homework for tonight. I look around at the whole class. Everyone has a blank look—this should be very interesting.

HUMM?

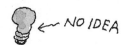
← NO IDEA

CHAPTER 2
A FAIR TO REMEMBER

On the bus ride home, we're deep in thought. We're all pretty fair-minded.

I think of all the fairs I've ever been to . . . one. It was the County Fair. It had a rodeo, and a bunch of cowboys riding bulls. Maybe I could put two horns on my dog, Tailspin.

FERRIS WHEEL

DRAGON'S NECK

ROLLER COASTER

VIKING SHIP

LAZY SUSAN

There was also a Ferris wheel. Plus there were crazy rides, cotton candy machines, corn-dog stands, and lots more. I don't think my class can do any of that stuff.

ELEPHANT EAR

COTTON CANDY

CORN DOG

SNOW CONE

JELLY BEAN

386

The fair organizers gave blue ribbons to both the cows and the cabbages. I know the difference between them, but that's about all.

It's going to be a long night of homework.

CHAPTER 3
UNFAIR

When I get home, I watch a video—*My Fair Lady*. It doesn't help much. Then I listen to the weather report...fair with a chance of showers. I've got fairs on the brain. Train fares, plane fares, bus fares, pharaohs, and good fairies.

I fall asleep watching a Ferris wheel go around. Suddenly I'm at a fair. I'm walking down the midway. It has a lot of booths.

I walk up to one. It's an alligator-kissing booth. No thanks. At the next booth, I get to slam-dunk an elephant into a basketball hoop.

Then there's a booth to bob for piranhas. If you survive that, you get to wrestle a bear. There are also booths for throwing marshmallows at balloons and for floating feathers in milk bottles. So far, I have not won anything.

GRRRR

Suddenly I'm in a gigantic fish bowl. Kids are trying to win me. They're throwing ping-pong balls that are bouncing all around. This is not fun. So I climb out of the bowl and go to buy a hotdog. But it's Tailspin in a bun.

MARS

PING!
PING!
PING!

PING-PONG BALLS →

HOT DOG

Then I buy some cotton candy, but it's made of real cotton. I wake up and see that I'm chewing on my pillow.

CHAPTER 4
MIRROR, MIRROR ON THE WALL . . .

On the school bus, everyone is excited. I think that they all have ideas, but no one's telling. They're waiting for class.

"Alright," says Mrs. Green. "Who has an idea for our class booth?"

Every hand shoots up. Penny raises two.

"Do you have an idea, Penny?"

"A kissing booth!" puckers Penny.

"YUCK! That won't make too much money," says Eric. "And besides, it's unsanitary!"

← GERMS
(EXACT SIZE)

Mrs. Green calls on Freddy.

"A bakery booth. I'll bake a lot of apple turnovers, and we'll sell them. We'll have a fast turnover," jokes Freddy.

"Possible," says Mrs. Green.

"Let's have a cakewalk," says Derrick.

"Great," says Freddy. "Then I'll bake a cake."

Eric waves his hand. "I'll get a crystal ball and tell the future."

"You can't tell the future," sneers Doris.

"I knew you would say that," smiles Eric.

CATERPILLAR CHIC

PAPER BALL → ○   GOLF BALL → ○   RUBBER BALL → ○   EYE-BALL → ⊙

"What about a basketball shoot?" says Randy.

"No way," says Eric. "Those fifth graders are too good, and they'll win all of our prizes."

"We could shoot meatballs instead," says Freddy.

HANDMADE PAPER BALLS →

"Too messy," I say. "What about a dunking tank?"

There's silence in the room. Mrs. Green turns and writes all the ideas on the board.

KISSING BOOTH
BAKERY BOOTH
CAKEWALK
FORTUNE-TELLER
BASKETBALL SHOOT
DUNKING TANK

SUGGESTION BOX

"Let's vote," she says.

The dunking tank idea wins hands down—or hands up.

"But who will we dunk?" asks Mrs. Green.

Everyone looks at her.

"No way!" says Mrs. Green.

ANY VOLUNTEERS?

Then everyone looks at me.

"I catch colds so easily," I announce. "What about dunking doughnuts?"

"I could bake the doughnuts," says Freddy.

"It was your idea," says Penny.

"Scared?" sneers Eric.

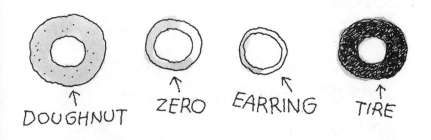

DOUGHNUT ZERO EARRING TIRE

I notice that everyone's staring at me.

"Me scared?" I squeak. "Not a chance."

"Then you will do it," says Eric.

"On one condition," I say.

"What's that?" asks Mrs. Green.

"You have to use ping-pong balls," I say with a smile.

"OK," says Mrs. Green. "Let's get to work."

WHAT NOISE DOES A MOUSE MAKE?
(CIRCLE ONE)

1. ROAR
2. SQUEAK
3. TWEET

ANSWER ON PAGE 406

CHAPTER 5
THE BETTER MOUSETRAP

ROCK

THE FIRST MOUSETRAP

The whole class pitches in and starts building the dunking booth. It's a lot of fun!

We get a plastic pool and fill it with water. So far, so good. We attach a chair to a hinged platform held up by a stick. Then we tie a cord around the stick and attach the other end to the spring of a mousetrap. Bingo!

"BINGO" IS THE NAME OF:
(CIRCLE ONE)

1. A LITTLE CAR
2. A GAME
3. A LARGE BIRD

ANSWER ON PAGE 411

We hit the trap. The spring snaps forward. It jerks the rope that pulls the stick, which drops the platform, and whoever is sitting in the chair falls into the water. *Splash!*

THE DUNKEE

HINGE

④

STICK

① PING-PONG BALL

③

② STRING

⑤

DON'T FORGET TO ADD WATER.

Hey, that'll be me. I'll be dropping into the water. Oh, me and my bright ideas! I don't even know how to swim. I better learn . . . fast.

SHARK

SNACK

CHAPTER 6
AQUA-PHOBIA!

I've always been afraid of the water. I'd rather stand on land than sink in the drink. It's fine for fish, but it's not my wish. But now, I have to learn how to swim.

My mom signs me up and takes me down to the public swimming pool. It's big! And it's full of water! It's six feet deep. Maybe I should go home and grow. I'll come back when I'm eight feet tall.

6 FEET

3 FEET (ALMOST)

ANSWER: SQUEAK

A nice lady comes over. She's got a whistle and a clipboard.

"I'm Miss Titanic, your swim instructor," she says.

"I want to miss this *Titanic*," I mutter.

"What?" she asks.

"Uh, nice to meet you, Miss Titanic," I reply.

QUACK.

"You must be Hubie," she says with a smile.

"Do I have to be?" I answer.

"You're right on time for your lesson," she says, checking her clipboard.

"Can I wait a couple of years?" I ask.

"Are we a little afraid of the water?" she laughs.

"Not if it's in a cup," I say.

"Just pretend that the pool is a big cup," she replies.

"I'm not that thirsty," I say, as she puts water wings on each of my arms.

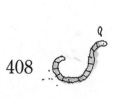

"Let's start off in the shallow end," she says, taking my hand.

"Any puddle is fine," I say.

"Come on, Hubie." She leads me down the steps into the pool. The water is very wet.

TOWELS

"Now duck, Hubie," she says.

"Quack, quack."

"No. Duck down," she laughs.

I shut my eyes, hold my breath, and duck down.

Phew! Waaaf! Schlurp!

"Now was that so bad?" she asks.

"Actually, it wasn't," I sigh.

"Now duck and open your eyes under the water."

"My eyeballs will drown," I protest.

"No, they won't. First, take a deep breath and hold it."

WOW!

ANSWER: A GAME

I keep my eyes open and they don't drown. I can actually see underwater. Maybe I have X-ray vision. I feel like a superhero... POOLMAN!

Anyway, in my first lesson I also learn to float. I'm a good floater. Maybe one day I can win an Olympic gold medal in floating. But more important, I'm almost ready for the carnival.

CHAPTER 7
FAIR-WEATHER FRIENDS

The whole school yard is alive with activity. Each class is putting up a booth. There's a ring toss, a baseball pitch, a basketball throw, a Frisbee fling, a tiddlywinks flip, and a lob the blob. There's even a turtle race. Why didn't I think of that?

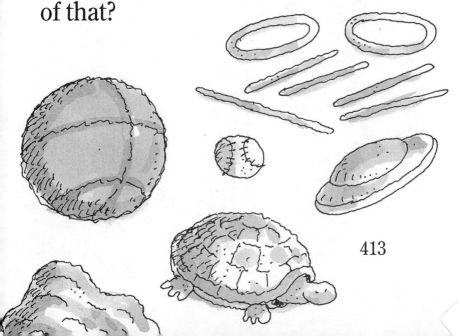

413

There's a wheel of fortune, a fortune-teller, and a telescope. You can see the future for a dollar, or the full moon for fifty cents, or a quarter moon for a quarter.

There's going to be a pie-eating contest. Freddy will probably win that. There's also a jelly bean contest. If you guess the number of jelly beans in a big jar, you can win a pair of Rollerblades.

"Every booth has a name," says Mrs. Green. "So what's the name of ours?"

"What about Dip the Drip?" replies Penny.

The rest of the class keeps on yelling out names.

"Spill the Pill," giggles Doris.

"Wet the Pet," grins Randy.

"Drown the Clown," laughs Derrick.

"Hey, that's me you're talking about!" I shout.

YOU'RE ALL WEIRD.

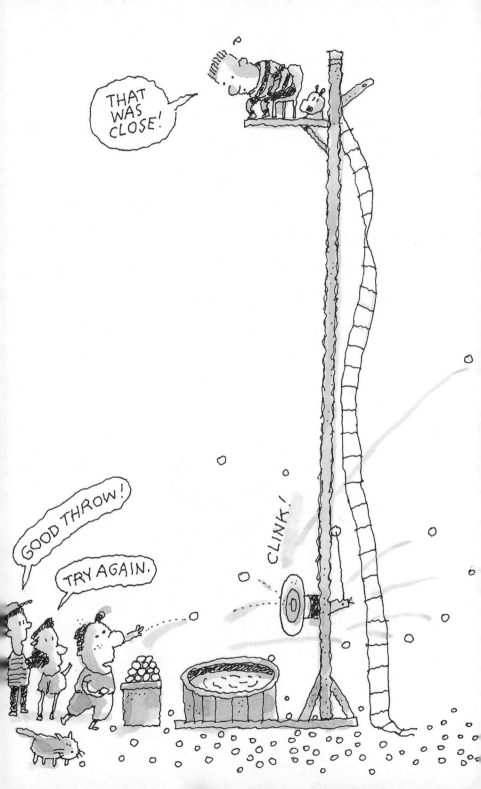

"What about Dunk the Skunk!" laughs Freddy.

"Hey!" I say.

"Dunk the Punk!" they all shout out together.

"I have it," I say, putting on my water wings and flexing my arms. "What about Dunk the Hunk!"

CHAPTER 8
IN THE SWIM

Well, it's Friday. The carnival is tonight. Are people that go to carnivals called *carnivores*? Everyone's very excited to see the Daredevil Diver. That's me. But it's more like the Dubious Diver.

A CARNIVORE IS:

1. A MEAT-EATER.

2. A CAR THAT RUNS ON GARLIC.

3. A TREE THAT GROWS IN WISCONSIN.

ANSWER ON PAGE 425

COLD
FEET →  ←THERMOS

I must admit that I'm getting cold feet. It could be very chilly tonight. The water could be freezing. I could get *hypo-thermos* or frostbite.

ICE

I go into the principal's office and ask Mr. Bender if he'll sit in for me. He says that he won't because at the County Fair he got hit with a pie during a charity event.

421

For the rest of the day, kids are wisecracking jokes at me.

"Taking the big plunge tonight, eh, Hubie?"

"You'll be a titanic success," someone chimes in.

"You'll make a big splash tonight!" another kid laughs.

They're getting me down in the dumps. I have fair-weather friends.

HUBIE CUT-OUT

TRACE THIS PAGE.

BE CAREFUL.

CUT HERE. FOLLOW THE DOTTED LINE.

PASTE HUBIE ON YOUR BOOK OR YOUR T-SHIRT.

I'm not ready for this!

I need six more years of swimming lessons.

"And besides, Hubie, you're the original hunk!" a bunch of kids yell.

That's funny because I feel more like the original junk.

CHAPTER 9
IN THE HOT SEAT

I have a sinking feeling as the carnival draws near. Mom drives me to school in the van. I'm taking 42 towels. I bought a fluorescent bathing suit so the rescue helicopter can spot me in the water. And I have three sets of water wings.

425

We pull right up to the carnival. I step out of the van and into a row of lights. It's like Academy Award night. I slowly walk down the aisle. All eyes are on me. I come to our booth, which we finally named, "The Big Dipper."

I take off my bathrobe, put on my three sets of water wings, flex, and climb the ladder to the chair. It's high up here. I'm *fair-in-height*.

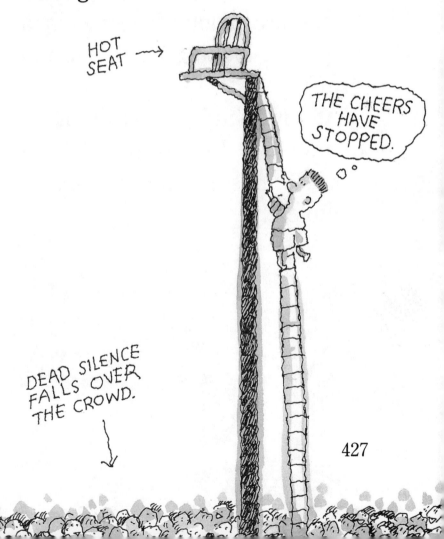

HOT SEAT →

THE CHEERS HAVE STOPPED.

DEAD SILENCE FALLS OVER THE CROWD.

I can see over most of the carnival.

Penny's selling tickets like crazy. Freddy's eating pie. And Randy's counting jelly beans. There are a lot of people in a long line, looking up to see me drown.

All my friends are at the front of the line. Eric is the first to try. He misses the mousetrap completely.

Derek and Doris get closer, but I am still high and dry. Freddy tries with blueberry pie all over his face. He misses, too.

Then the rest of the third grade takes a shot. I was smart to use ping-pong balls.

The tension mounts as ball after ball bounces off the trap, but each is too light to spring it. I make it through the fourth and fifth graders.

We're making a fortune and I'm still a dry guy in the sky!

CHAPTER 10
THE SLAM DUNK

Now the teachers start trying to sink me. Miss La Note, my music teacher, sings and misses.

Then Miss Swamp, my art teacher, draws a blank when she throws.

Even, Ms. Pluggins, the new computer teacher, takes a shot and short-circuits.

Finally, Mr. Bender buys a chance. I think he remembered that I was the guy who hit him with the pie at the County Fair! He misses, too. PHEW!

DETERMINED LOOK →

GREAT FORM

PRINCIPAL

LOOK AT THAT WIND-UP.

SINCE YOU'RE THE PRINCIPAL, YOU CAN CROSS THE LINE.

ACE

USED TO BE A BALLET DANCER

433

I'm feeling really good. I've beat the system. No one is in line anymore. I do a little victory dance on my chair.

FAN OF THE BALLET

DA DAAAA!

THE BIG DIPPER

I have a big, dry smile. Just as I am getting ready to climb down, I see something moving by the mousetrap.

Oh, no! A mouse!

INTERESTING.

The little rodent puts one foot on the trap and —WHAM! I'm in the water, and so is the mouse! He's a pretty good swimmer.

The water is not so cold. In fact, it's kind of fun. Everyone applauds as the mouse and I swim around.

We're the hit of the school carnival and even get our picture taken for the paper. I hope we're on the front page. The headline will probably read: BIG AND LITTLE DIPPERS.

WHAT FOOD DO MICE LOVE THE MOST?

1. WATERMELON
2. CHEESE
3. JELLY BEANS

436

ANSWER ON PAGE 439

Well, I continue with my swimming lessons. Last Friday, I did a cannonball off the diving board. I haven't seen the mouse at the pool, though. I think he went to the Mouse Olympics in Mouse-cow. Hey, maybe one day I'll win a gold medal, too.

LOOK OF CONFIDENCE.

FIRST AID KIT JUST IN CASE.

438

As it turns out, Randy's guess was the closest to the number of jelly beans and he won the Rollerblades. Freddy won the eating contest. He said it was as easy as pie. And we ended up raising enough money to get a fairly well-known author to come and visit our school.

ANSWER: CHEESE

If Your Dog Could Talk, What Would He Tell You?

TAYLOR-MADE TALES

THE DOG'S SECRET

by ELLEN MILES

SCHOLASTIC

New teacher Mr. Taylor can make up a great story using any five things his students choose. Give him a dog, a boat, a tennis ball, a playing card, and a necklace, and Mr. Taylor tells an exciting tale of a young girl who teaches her dog to talk and of the adventures they share.